2009,
HAPPY
BIRTHDAY
DAVID!
Love,
Aunt Amy

Big Rig

Grader Kat

Jack Truck

Monster Truck Max

Izzy Ice Cream Truck

Ice Cream

Tow Truck Ted

Simon & Schuster Books for Young Readers
An imprint of Simon & Schuster
Children's Publishing Division
1230 Avenue of the Americas
New York, New York 10020
Copyright © 2008 by Jon Scieszka
TRUCKTOWN and
JON SCIESZKA'S TRUCKTOWN and design
are trademarks of JRS Worldwide, LLC.
All rights reserved, including the right of
reproduction in whole or in part in any form.
SIMON & SCHUSTER
BOOKS FOR YOUNG READERS is
a trademark of Simon & Schuster, Inc.

Book design by Dan Potash
The text for this book is set in Truck King.
The illustrations for this book
are digitally rendered.
Manufactured in China
1 0 9 8 7 6 5 4 3 2
CIP data for this book is available
from the Library of Congress.
ISBN-13: 978-1-4169-4133-0
ISBN-10: 1-4169-4133-9

Characters and environments
developed by the

dESiGN
garage

David Shannon · Loren Long · David Gordon

To my pre-K Trucktown pals:
Allie, Angela, Ayinde, Bea, Caleb, Caitlin, Camilla,
Danny, Gregory, Henry, Jasmine, Laura, Lukas,
Malcolm, Martin, Mira, William, Yosef, Amileon, Claire,
Conor, Eli, Gabriela, Gerard, Iman, Julian, Kade,
Kennedy, Laura, Maxine, Michael, Mollie, Roman, Ryan,
Ruby, Sofia, and their wonderful teachers Marie and
Rose, Idalis and Jenny, Meriss and Aida.
—J. S.

ILLUSTRATION CREW

Executive producer

Keytoon INC.
in association with
ANIMAGIC S. L.

Creative Supervisor
Sergio Pablos

Drawings by
Juan Pablo Navas

Color by
Isabel Nadal

Art director
Dan Potash

SMASH! CRASH!

written by
Jon Scieszka

Jon Scieszka's
TRUCKTOWN

SIMON & SCHUSTER BOOKS FOR YOUNG READERS

New York   London   Toronto   Sydney

Jack Truck.

Dump Truck Dan.

Best friends.

Jack and Dan.

A shadow falls.
A big voice calls:

"HEY, YOU
TWO..."

Jack and Dan hit the road.
"Uh-oh."
"Got to go!"

Jack and Dan charge
Cement Mixer Melvin.

"Melvin!" calls Jack. "Time to smash!"
"Melvin!" yells Dan. "Time to crash!"

But Melvin is busy.
"No. I can't get messy.
I'm mixing,
mixing, mixing."

Jack signals Dan
and they ...

"You mixed it all," says Melvin.
"You also made a mess."

A clank. A rumble.
It must mean trouble.

"HEY, YOU TWO.
I WANT YOU."

Jack and Dan step on the gas.
"Uh-oh."
"Got to go."

Jack and Dan roll up to Monster Truck Max.
"Hey, Max," says Jack. "Help us smashing!"
"Yeah, Max," says Dan. "Help us crashing!"

But Max is awfully busy.

"Sorry, guys. No can do. Got to stack these barrels by two."

"Aw, don't be such a four-wheeler dud," says Jack. "Come on and ..."

"WoW,"
says Max.

"Smacked,
whacked, . . .
and stacked
to the max!"

Suddenly there's a
weird voice calling.
"Oh no," says Jack. "It's—"

"Do you want an ice cream?"

"It's Izzy!" says Dan.
"Not now, Izzy," says Jack.
Jack and Dan speed away.

They spot Gabriella Garbage
Truck and Grader Kat.
"Kat and Gabby!" says Jack.
"Smash and crash?" asks Dan.

But the girls are very busy. "My proper name is Gabriella," says Gabby, "and we are playing pirates."

"We'll play too," says Jack. "We are pirates who . . ."

"A perfect pirate fort," says Kat.

"Fabulous," says Gabby.

That shadow grows LARGER.
That voice calls LOUDER.

"HEY, YOU TWO.
I WANT
YOU.

I WANT
YOU TO ..."

Jack and Dan try to
race away, but . . .
"Oh no."
"No go."

It's Wrecking Crane Rosie.
Rosie is huge.
Rosie is strong.
Rosie booms,

"FOLLOW ME."

"Where is she taking us?"
"I don't know."

"Are we in trouble?"
"I don't know."

"What will she do to us?"
"I don't know."

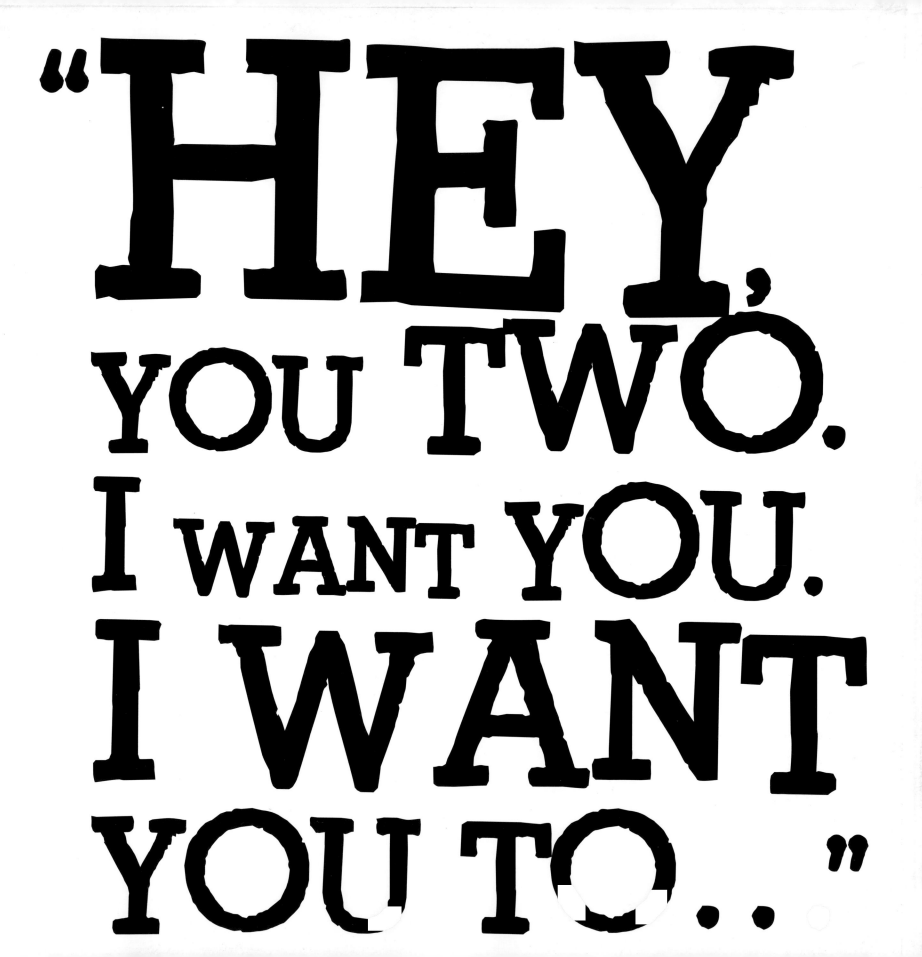

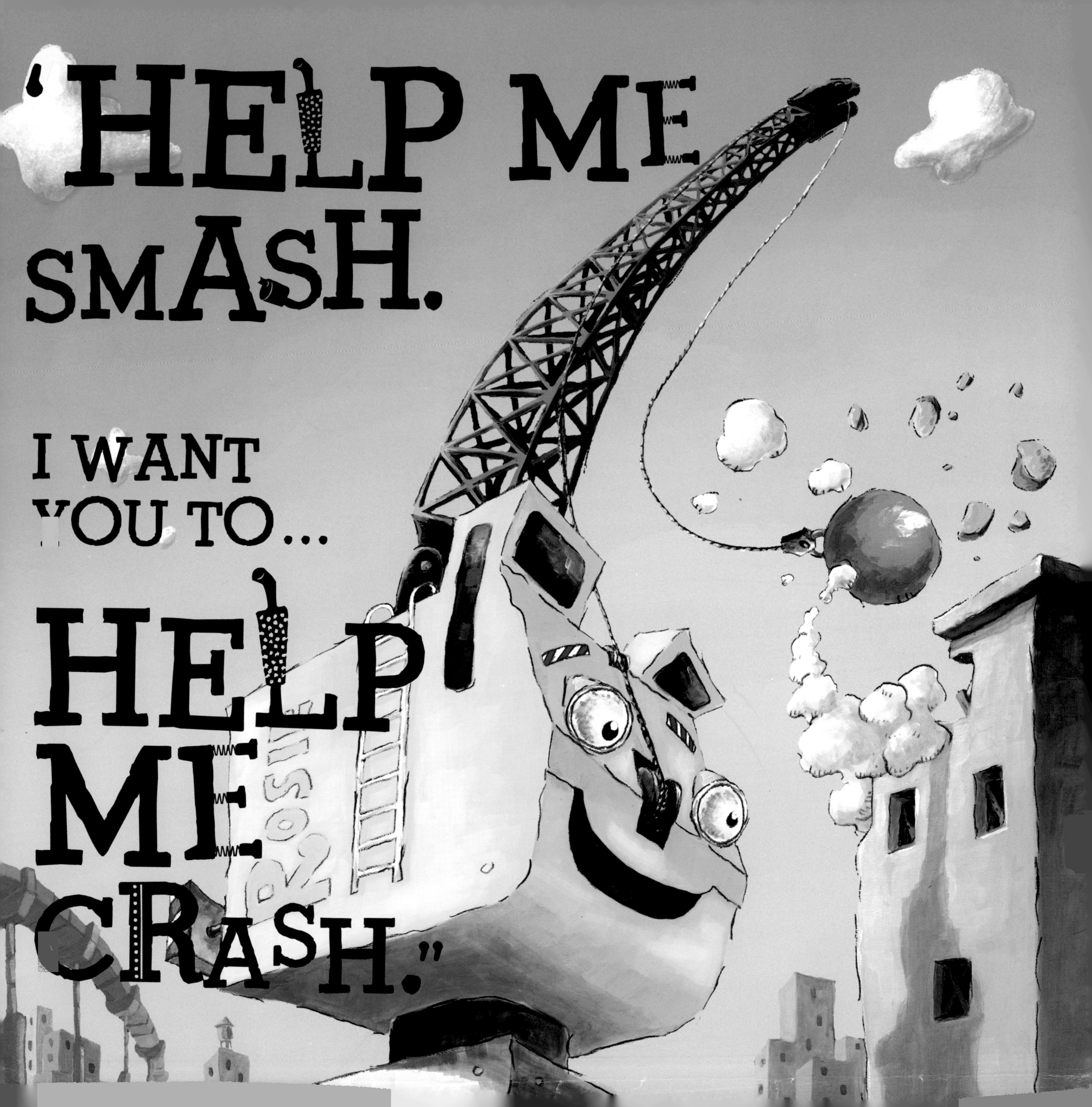
"HELP ME SMASH.
I WANT YOU TO...
HELP ME CRASH."
ROSIE

"Ohhhhh," says Dan.
"That's what you wanted?"
"We can do that," says Jack.
"We love to . . ."